Clean Break

Tammy Cohen

BLACK SWAN

TRANSWORLD PUBLISHERS
61–63 Uxbridge Road, London W5 5SA
www.transworldbooks.co.uk

Transworld is part of the Penguin Random House group of companies
whose addresses can be found at global.penguinrandomhouse.com

First published in Great Britain in 2017 by Black Swan
an imprint of Transworld Publishers

A CIP catalogue record for this book
is available from the British Library.

ISBN
9781784162917

Typeset in 12/16pt Stone Serif by Falcon Oast Graphic Art Ltd.
Printed and bound by Clays Ltd, Bungay, Suffolk.

Penguin Random House is committed to a sustainable
future for our business, our readers and our planet. This book
is made from Forest Stewardship Council® certified paper.

Clean Break

This is what you said:
It's not you, it's me.
You said:
I love you but I'm not in love with you.
You said:
I just need space.
You said:
Kids adapt.

This is what you did not say:
I'm sleeping with someone else.

But we made vows.
And I intend to keep them.
Till death do us part.

Chapter One

'There's no ham! Mum, Ben ate all the ham.'

'I did not! I haven't been near the fridge.'

'Liar!'

'Enough now, you two.'

Kate glares at her two children, trying to look stern.

'Look, this sneaking food from the kitchen all the time has got to stop. Yesterday there were no crisps for packed lunches. And last week you ate all the KitKats.'

'But I didn't . . .' Amy's eyes are round with outrage, but Kate ignores her.

'I don't care who did what, just pack it in. OK?'

The kids leave the room, still arguing. Kate hears Ben's heavy footsteps pounding up the stairs. When did he get so big? Almost a man now. She selects a playlist from her phone and slots it into the speaker. Still such a thrill to be able to listen to what she wants, when she wants.

She hums along as she washes up the breakfast things. She's forgotten about the missing ham.

When was the last time she felt this happy?

The blaring of her ringtone cuts through the music. Kate dries her hands on her jeans. She hasn't been able to fit into these jeans for at least two years. Being able to wear them again feels like an omen, like the start of a new life.

'Hi, Mel,' she says, tucking the phone under her ear.

'Are you drunk?' asks Mel. 'You sound drunk.'

'No, just washing up,' says Kate. 'Having a dance.'

'God help us. I've seen you dance.'

Kate laughs. After so long living with Jack and his constant put-downs she has grown to hate being teased but with Mel she doesn't mind so much. One of the perks of being best friends for twenty-five years.

'How's it going?' Mel wants to know.

Kate knows that what Mel is really asking is how are things with Jack. She glances at the kitchen door, which still has a hole where Jack punched it. Then she walks over and closes it – to be on the safe side. Then she sighs.

'Oh, you know. One step at a time. At least it is all in the open now. He's getting it at last. That it's over.'

'But you still haven't told him about . . .'

Again, Kate glances at the door. Even though she knows Jack isn't there.

Old habits die hard.

'God, no. He'd go mad. You know what he's like. It's early days. We still need to work out the details of the split. Where he will live. How often he will have the kids. How much he will give us. God, I wish we had the money for a clean break. If only he could get his own place. Then we could start living our own lives and I wouldn't have to tiptoe around him all the time.'

'Just take care, hun, all right?'

After the phone call, Kate tries to get back to the good mood of before, but Jack is like a black cloud hanging over the kitchen. How strange to think that there was once a time when just the thought of him made her light up inside.

She thinks about the first time they saw this house. Her and Jack. The kitchen was all brown then. It was really ugly.

'I'll make it nice for you, I promise,' Jack had said.

That first night after they moved in she sat on the stairs and cried. Refused to set foot in the kitchen. But he was as good as his word, coming home from work and changing into old jeans to slap on fresh paint and chip away at manky tiles. It wasn't perfect. Jack was always in such a hurry. And then there was that temper of his. The shouting that went on when things went wrong. Never at her, mind.

Not back then, anyway.

There's a noise on the stairs and Kate's chest gets tight. Silly. She knows it isn't Jack. Just one of the kids coming down. Still, it takes a while for her heartbeat to get back to normal.

The thing is, they were happy in those early years. Broke, of course. But that didn't matter so much then. They had rows, like everyone does. But making up was always such fun. Then came the kids. And there was never enough time. Or sleep. Or money. And Jack was always in such a bad mood.

She had tried. No one could say she hadn't.

And now she is entitled to a little happiness.

Her little bit of happiness is called Tom. Thinking about her new boyfriend Tom gives her a little glow of pleasure. They have been seeing each other for a few weeks now. In secret. Everything about him feels new and unspoiled. The way he says her name as if he is rolling it around on his tongue like fine wine. The feel of his fingers on her skin.

But now she sees Jack's face in her mind, and

guilt rolls over her like a wave. She reminds herself that she and Jack are separated now. She has been upfront and honest.

To a point.

With someone as quick to anger as Jack, there is a limit to how honest you can be.

Amy bursts into the kitchen.

'Have you seen my yellow top? It went in the wash ages ago and now I can't find it.'

Kate doesn't like the way Amy speaks to her these days. Amy does not want her mum and dad to split up. Kate can understand that. And it doesn't help that Jack puts the blame completely on her.

'It's not what I want,' he'd told the kids when they first broke the news three days ago.

Kate had been upset by that. She had wanted them to put on a united front – for the sake of the children. Instead, she's been painted as the bad guy. After everything she did to try to save the relationship.

'I have no clue where it is,' she tells her daughter.

The words come out sounding harsher than she meant and Amy turns on her heel and flounces out, slamming the door behind her.

Kate stares after her and sighs.

Kids adapt, she reminds herself. They will

come round, sooner or later. And it is not as if Ben and Amy are little any more. At fifteen and fourteen they are so wrapped up in themselves they hardly notice anyone else. She has been a great mum to them. Just as she was a great wife to Jack – until now.

She deserves to be happy.

A Taylor Swift track comes on. Jack could never bear this song and would always switch it off if it ever came on the car radio.

Kate turns up the music as loud as it will go.

Chapter Two

JACK: Wednesday evening,
three days after the split

I have a book open in front of me but still I watch you from the corner of my eye. You have lost weight. But the thing is, you didn't need to. You always looked lovely to me.

I remember the first time I saw you. Your red hair was tied up in a ponytail and you had leggings on and trainers. You and your friend Mel had come straight from a step class at the gym. Called in for one drink before heading home, you said.

Just one drink. That's all it takes to change the course of a life.

Two lives.

I was with my brother, Matt. 'That's the one,' I told him. 'That's her.'

You hadn't even had a shower after your class. I could smell you. I could always smell you.

Some people don't believe in love at first sight. They think love is something that creeps up on you softly, like old age. Until one day it strikes you – 'Oh, *this* must be love.' I pity those people. When I saw you across the pub, love hit me around the head like a sock full of ball bearings.

After that, it was as if I had always known you. We did everything together. Like there was an invisible chain linking one to the other. I told you I loved you a week after we met. And moved in with you after a month. You weren't a hundred per cent sure at first, and Mel had her nose put out of joint when I was there every morning in my dressing gown. But she soon gave up and moved out of your flat. And then it was just the two of us. Always.

How can you have forgotten all that?

You glance up and I instantly look away. Then I am cross with myself. As if it makes the slightest bit of difference. You can't see me. I don't exist for you any more.

'Ben, how many times do I need to tell you? No texting at the table.'

When you frown, a deep line appears down your forehead. You used to hate your lines and stand in front of the mirror stretching your skin back so it was as smooth as it used to be. But to me, your lines were beautiful. A map of the journey we have been on together over the last sixteen years.

'You can talk,' says Ben. 'Your phone is almost glued to your hand.'

Ben shouldn't be cheeking you. In the past, I would have jumped in. Made him say sorry and show some respect. But now I sit here saying nothing.

Your cheeks flush pink as you slam the food down on to the table.

Amy rolls her eyes.

'Spaghetti bolognese again. What a surprise. Not.'

When did she get so rude? I wait for you to tell her off, but you bite your lip instead, as if you are trying to keep the words in.

Ben and Amy are sitting on the near side of the table, so you have to squeeze past them. You are much thinner now but our table has always been too big for the space. Some sauce spills from your bowl as you slide into your seat, and you put your head in your hands.

'I hate this bloody kitchen,' you say. 'I've always hated it. As soon as I get paid I'm going to get the whole thing re-done. New cupboards, new layout, new colour scheme. Everything white. I wish I'd done that from the start. Only your father insisted he knew best.'

It feels like a blade passing in between my ribs. When I think of how hard I worked. After eight hours sitting in traffic jams – putting up with rude passengers in my cab who think it's my fault when the lights turn red or we get stuck behind a learner driver. And having to smile and be pleasant, even after breaking my back lifting their huge cases into the boot of the cab for a measly one pound tip. After a day of that I would come home and be straight into stripping and sanding and painting.

And all for you.

I curl my fingers into a fist and press until the nails make dents in the palms of my hand.

Ben is talking about something that happened at school. He claims his maths teacher picked on him, when in fact it was his friend who was doing the talking, not him. 'It is so unfair,' he says. 'It's always me who gets the blame.'

I am not really listening. Instead I am rewinding our lives like a movie, trying to pinpoint the exact moment things started to change. Where is the trap door I failed to notice that dropped me from the life we had before into this living hell? Where are the signs I failed to see? But no matter how I rake over the past, I cannot find an answer.

There is only before. And after.

We were right here in this kitchen. It came out of nowhere. I had walked in and turned the music down a little. Not off, just down. It was too loud to hear myself think. You were chopping onions with your back to me. And I saw you freeze as if someone had hit pause. Then, without turning around, you said, 'I want a divorce.'

You still had your back to me, and I thought I might not have heard right. So I asked you what you had said. I was half smiling because I was about to say, 'I thought for a moment you said you wanted a divorce.' Then you sat down and you said all those things. 'It's not you, it's me.' 'I love you but I'm not in love with you.' 'We can still be friends.'

And I couldn't take it in. I still can't take it in.

'Mum,' Amy says, 'I keep hearing weird noises in the night. They wake me up. How am I expected to go to school if I can't get any sleep?'

'What kind of noises?' you ask.

She shrugs.

'Creaking and scratching.'

'It will just be Sid, prowling around,' you say.

'So how do you explain that Sid was fast asleep on my bed at the time?'

Sid is the cat. He is not supposed to sleep on the beds, but you don't protest.

'In that case, it must be the squirrels back again,' you say, and sigh. 'That's all we need.'

There's a buzzing sound coming from somewhere.

'Don't look at me,' says Amy.

You jump up and dive for your phone, which is on the kitchen worktop.

'So I can't use my phone at mealtimes, but it is all right for you to keep checking your texts every five minutes,' says Ben.

'It's not every five minutes,' you say.

You are trying to sound cross, but I see how you are trying to hide a secret smile as you read what is on your screen.

A nugget of anger sits in my gut, solid as a gallstone.

Chapter Three

Kate tries to hold on to her good mood as she lets herself in through the front door, but there is something about the air in the hallway that seems heavy and solid. It gets in her nose and mouth and makes it hard to breathe. She feels the glow she has been carrying with her fade away until there is nothing left.

She used to love her house, but now when she comes in her chest gets tighter and there's a dull ache in the pit of her stomach.

She hangs up her coat on a hook in the hall and bends down to line up Ben's trainers, which he has kicked off across the hallway. She normally likes this half-hour on a Thursday between her getting home from her job on the reception desk at the health clinic and the kids arriving back late from football and drama. It's a time when she can relax and make a cup of tea and enjoy a few moments of calm. But today she feels as if ants are

13

crawling around inside her and she can't settle.

The feeling is worse when she goes into the living room, like something prickling on the skin at the back of her neck. There is something about the room that isn't right. But she can't work out what it is.

She sinks down into the soft cushions of the sofa and allows herself to think about Tom. How he looked at her when she snatched a couple of hours to go and meet him last night. She told the kids she was going to the gym. Afterwards, Amy looked at her long and hard and said, 'Since when do you wear make-up to go to the gym?'

Kate thinks about how gentle Tom is. How kind. How he gave money to the *Big Issue* seller and stopped to have a chat.

Jack never gives money to people on the streets. He says they will either smoke it or drink it. Tom says if he was sleeping rough, he might well take up drinking and drugs, too.

Tom has dark hair that curls over his shirt collar. Sometimes he tries to flatten it down with gel but it always springs up by the end of the night. He has a long, thin nose that looks like someone pinched it at the end. He has green eyes, and Kate pretends to be annoyed that his lashes are longer than her own.

There is a sound by the door and Kate jumps,

but it is just Sid slinking in with his tail held up high behind him.

'You scared me, Sidney,' says Kate, stroking the huge tabby.

Sid purrs and leaps up on to Kate's lap, knocking a GCSE Science text book off the coffee table. Now Kate sees what is not right about the room. When she left this morning the book was on the floor where Ben had dropped it. She had been in too much of a rush to clear it up. She remembers feeling cross about how little help Ben was giving her around the house.

He must have come back at lunchtime and tidied up. Maybe he is finally learning.

A sharp knock on the front door startles her, until she remembers that Mel said she would call in on her way home from work.

As ever, her best friend blows in like a tornado, flinging her arms around Kate and almost knocking her off her feet.

'Tell me *everything*,' Mel says, her pale blue eyes wide in her round face.

They head into the kitchen. Suddenly, Kate feels much better. Lighter. Mel wants to smoke so they step outside into the back garden. Kate tells Mel about meeting Tom the night before. What they said. What they did. It is late afternoon and Kate raises her face to catch the last rays of the weak spring sun on her skin. She feels her good mood return.

'Good for you, hun,' says Mel. 'You have earned this. You haven't been happy for years.'

'Exactly,' says Kate. 'I can't tell you how hard I worked at being married, Mel. I gave Jack so many chances to put things right. But you know what he's like. He never listens. Just talks over you. And he always has to control everything. I tried and tried, but one day I just snapped.

'I was in here, preparing dinner and listening to music, and he walked in and turned it off. Just like that. Without even saying anything. I stood totally still for a moment, thinking, *In a minute, I will carry on as normal.* But then it was like a light going on in my brain, and I thought, *Enough now. I've had enough.* And I said, "I want a divorce."'

Mel nods over the top of her teacup and Kate feels something inside her grow looser, something she wasn't even aware had been clenched. It is so good to see Mel here. She avoids the house if she knows Jack is going to be around.

'I'm so proud of you,' Mel tells her. 'I know what a temper Jack has. It must have been scary to stand up to him like that. How is he taking everything?'

Kate shrugs.

16

'It's weird. He is so calm. I keep waiting for him to blow up like he did when I first told him, but he hasn't. He doesn't say anything at all. It freaks me out, if I'm honest.'

'Better than him ranting and raving,' says Mel. 'It must be strange, though, living in limbo like this. When is he moving into his own place?'

'I don't know. We keep out of each other's way. His stuff is here but he is usually out at work or staying with friends.'

'And how are the kids taking it?'

'Oh, they are angry with me. And hurt. Amy is not sleeping and hearing noises in the night. Ben tries to wind me up. Nicking food from the fridge. Being rude.'

'They will get over it.'

'I just wish I could fast-forward six months and this bit would all be over with,' says Kate. 'We are going to counselling tonight. Me and Jack. I am dreading it.'

Mel frowns. 'I don't get it. You and Jack have split up now. So why are you still going to counselling?'

'I wanted to stop,' says Kate. 'But Julie, the counsellor, thinks it will help make the break-up smoother. And Jack wants us to carry on going. I think he thinks I will change my mind.'

'Will you tell him about . . .?'

Kate scrunches up her features, pulling her chin right back into her neck.

'Course not. Do I look crazy?'

'Yes, when you're making that face!'

As their laughter tails off, Mel looks serious for once.

'Just be careful, hun. OK?'

Kate nods, but fear, like the tip of an ice-cold finger, is running down her spine.

Chapter Four

JACK: Thursday evening,
four days after the split

I have dressed with care. I am wearing the shirt
you bought me. Blue to match my eyes, you said.
You like the way it is tight in the upper arms
over my biceps. I keep myself in good shape. For
you. All for you.

I had a shower earlier this afternoon, and now
I spray myself with the aftershave you like. At
the top of the stairs I wait, listening for the television. Then I pad down in my socks, putting
my shoes on by the front door before letting
myself out. I need a drink before counselling.
Just one. To steady my nerves.

One turns into three. As it often does. But
that's all right.

We meet outside the counsellor's house. It's
a nice house. Semi-detached with purple slate
gravel in the front garden and a wisteria plant
framing the doorway. The first time we came
here you said this was your dream house. That
was when I still thought this was just a bad

patch in our marriage. I watched you take in the wide hallway with the sweeping staircase, and the huge square living room with golden floorboards and a real fireplace. I knew you were comparing it to our small, cosy terraced house. I knew you were blaming me for not giving you what Julie has. A pain started in my head that still bothers me now.

As always, Julie answers the door and leads the way past the living room to the little room at the back where she sees her clients. *Clients*. It makes us sound like we are at the bank asking about a loan, instead of trying to save our marriage.

We sit down on the boxy blue sofa, one at each end. You could park a bus in the space between us.

Julie sits in a chair opposite. She has brown hair that comes to her chin and swings when she talks, and her eyes are so close together she sometimes looks cross-eyed. Her tights always match her clothes. Today she has on a green jumper and skirt and tights of exactly the same colour. The first time we came she was wearing red all over, and you said afterwards that you thought she should have chosen a calmer colour.

'How have you two been?' Julie asks.

'Great,' you say, and I laugh.

'Interesting that your response is laughter,

Jack,' says Julie. 'Is that because it is funny or because you don't see how Kate could be feeling great?'

That is what she does. Picks apart every little thing you say or do like it's a faulty seam.

'I just can't see there's much that's great at the moment,' I say.

There's a low table in front of the sofa which is clear apart from a single box of tissues. Most weeks you make good use of that box.

Now I stare at the tissue box long and hard to avoid looking anywhere else.

Julie asks about the kids. You say they are angry with us both. But that isn't true. They are angry with you, and I point that out. Then she asks about living arrangements and you say things are not ideal, but you hope we can sort something out that suits us both. I stare at the box of tissues and press the nails of my right hand into the palm of my left hand and say nothing.

You say, 'You see, Julie? You see how he is? Talking to him is like getting blood from a stone.'

So Julie looks at me and asks, 'How about it, Jack? Do you have anything you would like to say to Kate?'

'Yes,' I say. 'I would like to ask Kate if she is

seeing someone else. I am not angry any more. I just want to know the truth.'

You make a tutting noise and shake your head. You and Julie look at each other. 'He's like a stuck record,' you tell her.

Julie turns to me, and I look at how her hair is swinging by her jaw so that I don't have to look into her eyes.

'You bring this up every week, Jack,' she says. 'And every week, Kate denies it.' Her voice is soft and she never raises it. Even when I lost it the first time we came here, she didn't raise her voice. She just quietly told me that, though she could see why I was upset, she would not put up with threats. She said that, if I carried on, I would have to leave the room.

She continues. 'Do you think you are so fixed on the idea that Kate has another man, because it is easier to accept that, than to accept that she is no longer in love with you? It is very easy in cases like this to look for someone or something to blame, rather than have to look at our own behaviour. Do you see that, Jack?'

She is looking at me intently with her nearly crossed-over eyes. I look back at the box of tissues so I don't have to see her any more, or see your face.

Because I know you are lying.

I count to ten in my head, nice and slow, and I imagine throwing a coconut against a wall as hard as I can. I hear it crack as it hits.

Chapter Five

KATE: Friday afternoon,
five days after the split

Kate is called in to see Alice, the practice manager at the health centre where she works.

'I am sorry,' she says, even before Kate has sat down.

Alice is sitting behind her desk. She has faded, strawberry-blonde hair, streaked with grey, which she is wearing in a plait. And pink cheeks that always look as if she has just come inside from somewhere very cold. She takes off her black-framed glasses and tips her head to one side. Her brown eyes are full of concern.

'It's so unlike you, Kate,' Alice says. 'All these years you have worked here, and this is the first complaint.'

'She was being so difficult,' Kate says. 'I'd offered her a three o'clock with Dr Davis, or a three-twenty with Dr Patel, but she kept insisting that only Dr Fox would do.'

'But Mrs Hayes is always difficult. And you are usually so good with her. What is going on? How are things at home?'

Kate can feel herself blushing. 'Fine. Well, not fine. But OK. Jack seems to have accepted that we are splitting up. It's just . . .'

But she cannot think of how to finish the sentence. She cannot put into words the strange atmosphere in the house, the creeping sense she has of things not being right. It should be a relief, now that everything is out in the open, but instead they all seem so on edge.

Tom calls her while she is waiting to catch a bus home from work. He wants to meet her.

'I can't. I need to be home for the kids.'

'Can't your husband . . .?'

'He's working.'

'Come on. It's Friday. They are old enough to do their own thing.'

Kate hesitates. She thinks about spending another evening at home, arguing with Amy. Then she imagines how it would feel to have Tom's arms around her.

'You've twisted my arm,' she tells him.

But all the time they are out together she feels something nagging at her like a mild toothache. Tom is funny and kind, but one time when she goes to the loo she almost walks past him when she comes back. She is so used to Jack, Tom seems like a stranger.

When he asks her to come back to his flat she says she has to get home. It is true, but it is not the entire truth. She has made excuses to her family in the past so she could stay out. She could do so again.

She hears the music from way down the street, blasting out through her living room window. When she bursts through the door she finds Amy and four friends from school, including a boy called Max, who she suspects is Amy's new boyfriend. She doesn't trust Max. He has hair that he sweeps to one side across his eyes, and he grins at her as if he is part of some big joke that she isn't in on. The place is trashed with crisp packets and Coke cans all over the floor, and even two bottles of beer. And when she goes into the kitchen Kate is sure she can smell cigarettes.

'Time to go,' she tells them, snatching Amy's phone from the speaker so that the music cuts out suddenly. The silence is brutal and two of Amy's friends giggle nervously.

After the teenagers have left, Amy bursts into tears.

'You just want to ruin my life,' she says. 'As if breaking up my family isn't bad enough. Now you don't want me to have friends either. I'm calling Dad.'

'He'll be driving,' says Kate. 'He won't pick up.'

Amy runs up to her room and slams the door. When Kate goes up to bed, Amy is still in there, refusing to talk. When Kate walks past the door of the box room, she turns her head away so she can't see all Jack's things. But she feels guilty all the same.

In the doorway of her bedroom she stops. Something is wrong. She looks around the room, which still feels so strange without Jack's shoes lined up neatly under the bed or a history book on the table on his side of the bed, with a bookmark keeping his place. Someone has been in here. She knows it.

Kate looks closely at the bed. She is always careful about making it in the mornings, tugging down the bottom corners of the duvet so it is completely smooth. Neatness has become a habit, a result of living with Jack all these years. But though the bed is made, with the duvet pulled up, it is creased, as though someone has been lying on it, and there is a dent in one of the pillows.

'Amy, get in here!' she yells.

'Why?'

'Just do it.'

Seconds later, Amy is standing in the doorway with her arms folded and a scowl on her face.

She looks heartbreakingly young, and Kate is flooded with sadness and doubt.

'Someone has been in my bed while I wasn't here. I need you to be honest with me, Amy. Was it you and Max?'

Amy's eyes grow wide.

'What? No. Ew. What do you take me for?'

'Well, who then?'

'No one. We stayed downstairs all the time. All of us.'

For a moment Kate wavers. Amy's outrage seems so real. Then she glances again at the dent in the pillow and her resolve hardens.

'I don't believe you. You're grounded this weekend.'

'You can't do that! I haven't done anything! It is so unfair.'

Amy's voice is becoming ever more shrill.

'And if you're not careful, you will be grounded the weekend after that, too,' adds Kate.

'You are literally the worst. I hate you.'

After Amy has rushed back to her room and slammed the door once again, Kate lies in bed and thinks of all the ways she could have handled things better. She should have talked to Amy quietly and calmly. Made sure she knew she wasn't in trouble. It was just such a shock, that's all. Amy is a child still. To think that she might have . . . Well, Kate doesn't want to think about it. That's the thing.

As the hours tick by without her being able to sleep, Kate lies in the dark and listens to the house creak and sigh. She tries to make herself think about Tom and how he looks at her, so she can find again the happiness of a few days ago. But every time she tries to picture his face, she sees Jack's instead. She sees his expression when he turned to her in Julie's counselling room and asked if she was seeing someone else.

Amy isn't the only one in the family telling lies.

Chapter Six

You are watching the television.

And I am pretending to watch the television, but really I am watching you watching the television.

Even from the side, I can see how hollow your cheeks have become, as if the air is being sucked out of them. There are black shadows under your eyes and you are chewing on a tiny piece of skin in the corner of your fingernail.

You do not look good.

There's a stupid show on the television. About couples meeting up to go on dates. It is all set in a restaurant. I wonder if it makes you think about our first date. I took you to a French place that had just opened. I was shocked when I saw the menu. It was the most expensive restaurant I had ever been to, but I let you think it was all the same to me.

'Have whatever you like,' I said. 'Have lobster, if you like.'

I chose that because it was the most expensive thing and I wanted you to see I couldn't care less about the price. Afterwards, you admitted you had never had lobster before and you only ordered it because I had suggested it. And you didn't even like it that much.

You can't have forgotten it all.

The ads come on and you jump up as if you have just thought of something. You go into the kitchen and I follow you there.

You drag a chair to the far wall and stand on it so you can reach the high kitchen cupboard where we keep the alcohol. Where *you* keep the alcohol. You reach behind the collection of odd bottles we have built up over the years – vermouth, Malibu, a strange yellow drink we brought back from holiday one year. You bring out the bottle of vodka we keep in the cupboard for whenever people come round. You are not normally a big drinker. This is unusual for you.

Getting yourself a glass, you pour a modest measure of vodka. Then you look at it for a moment and pour in a bit more. You open the freezer and take out an ice tray, which is mostly empty. 'Typical,' you say under your breath. Managing to get two cubes of ice out, you fetch a bottle of Coca-Cola from the fridge and pour some in. The bottle has been there a few days and there's no fizzing noise when it hits the ice.

You carry your drink back into the living room and sit back down on the sofa with your feet curled up underneath you. Then you take a big swig.

You frown, and take another.

Getting up suddenly, you storm back into the kitchen and get the bottle of vodka down again. You hold it under your nose and take a big sniff. Then you hold the bottle to your mouth and take a gulp.

'Ben!' Your shout is so loud your voice cracks. 'Ben! Come here!'

There's the sound of something heavy thundering down the stairs and Ben appears in the kitchen. He looks cross.

'I was in the middle of something,' he says. 'What's up?'

'This is what's up,' you say, pointing to the vodka.

He shrugs.

'I don't have a clue what you're talking about.'

'Someone has drunk the vodka and replaced it with water.'

'Well, don't look at me.'

'Are you really going to stand there and tell me it wasn't you? Haven't I raised you to tell the truth?'

32

'Truth? That's rich. Coming from you.'

'What's that supposed to mean? Ben, come back here!'

But Ben has already left the room. His feet thump on the stairs.

For a second you stand there with your mouth open as if you are about to call after him. Then you slump down into the chair, put your head in your hands and sob as if your heart is breaking.

Chapter Seven

KATE: Thursday evening,
eleven days after the split

How is it possible that it's Thursday again? The weeks seem to be rolling into one, and still nothing is getting better. Whoever said time is a healer was lying.

Kate waits for Jack outside Julie's front gate. The counsellor lives in the kind of house Kate has always dreamed of. She made the mistake of telling Jack that the first time they came here, when they were still together, still trying to 'save the relationship'. He never stopped going on about it. How ungrateful she was after all that he'd done to make their house a home. He said that was her all over, always complaining about something, always thinking someone else had the life she should have had. 'The grass is always greener somewhere else for you, isn't it?' he'd yelled at her on the way home.

Is he right? she thinks now. Is she too hard to please? Should she have settled for what she had? Put up with Jack and his black rages? At least then the kids might still be speaking to her.

She glances at Jack from the corner of her eye. He is wearing a black T-shirt and black jeans and his hair is neatly gelled. He has made an effort.

'I want to try a new approach this week,' says Julie, leaning forwards. She is wearing purple trousers and a purple cardigan done up all the way to the top.

'With all the stuff that has been going on, the last few sessions have been a bit negative, which isn't at all a surprise. So I think it would be really useful if we could restore a bit of balance. What I want you to do today is to each think of three things you used to like about each other.'

Kate closes her eyes. Takes a deep breath. This isn't what she wants to do. She wants to work out how to split up from Jack. Not to remember the things that brought them together.

But Julie is costing them £75 an hour. So there is no point in not doing what she says.

Jack goes first.

'I liked Kate's smile,' he says.

'Don't look at me and say it,' says Julie. 'I know it's hard but, if possible, I would like you to turn to Kate and say it directly to her.'

'I liked your smile,' says Jack. He is facing me, but he is addressing a point somewhere by my ear.

'Very good,' says Julie. 'What else?'

'I liked how patient she was with the kids. Never shouting at them. Not like now, with the bed and the vodka. She was a brilliant mum. And I liked the way she looked at me. She made me feel like I was the most important man in the world.'

Now Jack is finally looking at her, and Kate looks away, feeling the blood rushing to her cheeks. She is embarrassed, and there is something niggling in the back of her mind. Something she can't quite put her finger on.

'Kate?' says Julie.

Kate breathes in.

'I liked your confidence,' she tells Jack, forcing herself to meet his eyes.

'And I liked how you always took care of me. Well, I liked it at first, before it became suffocating.'

'Stick with positive things, please, Kate,' says Julie sternly.

'Sorry. I liked how you used to make me feel safe.'

Kate realizes now how much she has missed that feeling. Not that it has been very evident over the last few years. But there was a time when being with Jack was like wearing armour that meant no one could hurt her. *Until the*

36

person hurting you was Jack, says a voice in her head. But she dismisses it. Julie wants them to be nice about each other, and that's what she will do. Kate switches off the voice and stops trying to work out what is niggling at her. Instead she holds Jack's gaze, even though her face is now burning.

After the session Jack asks her if she wants a lift home, and she accepts. She has a car, but she only drives when she has to. Driving was always Jack's job.

Now they drive in silence, but the air in the car crackles with something alive. It is as if the counselling session has lit a flame that has burnt away the last few terrible years, sending them back to a time before the fights and the name-calling and the bitter things they both said.

'Shall we pop into the King's Head? Just for a quick one?' Jack asks.

And though it is Thursday and she should be home sorting the kids out, making sure they do their homework, and though she knows she definitely should not be going anywhere with Jack, she says yes. She is so tired. And now Julie has made her remember how it felt to have someone to look after her and to care about her being tired.

She has a glass of wine. And then another. And a third.

And on the way back to the house, Jack takes her hand, as if none of the last few weeks has happened.

'Oh,' says Amy, when she sees her parents come stumbling into the house together.

'Jesus Christ,' says Ben. 'Get a room, would you?'

But Kate sees the two of them exchange smiles before they head upstairs.

And because she is drunk, and because she is tired and weak and her thoughts are full of a rose-tinted past, Kate doesn't say no when Jack kisses her. And when he goes to the loo and she looks at her phone and sees seven missed calls from Tom and three texts, she switches her phone off altogether.

And when, later, Jack leads her upstairs to bed, she does not object.

Chapter Eight

JACK: Friday morning,
twelve days after the split

It is over. We are a family again.

I am giddy with relief.

For the first time in two weeks, I slept properly, and now I have woken up in my own bed, in my own room, and everything feels right again. I look up at the ceiling and it still has the thin crack in one corner. And straight ahead there is the picture of Amy and Ben as small children that I had printed on to canvas for your fortieth birthday last year. You cried. Remember?

I turn and watch you sleeping and think how beautiful you are.

When you wake up and find me watching you, your eyes grow wide, and there is a moment when you look almost scared. I smile and lean over to kiss you.

'It's only me,' I say.

You jump up, saying you are late for work, though the alarm has not yet gone off. I love how you are too embarrassed to meet my eye. It reminds me of when we first got together.

At breakfast, the kids are quiet. Looking from you to me and back again. Trying to guess what is going on but not wanting to ask. Amy catches my eye, and I wink at her. I feel like a million dollars. You leave for work early, saying you have stuff to do. I go with you to the door and give you a hug, but when I try to kiss you, you wriggle away, saying you have to rush. It doesn't worry me. I know you need time to process last night. But I also know that, like me, you can feel how right this is.

I text you on your way to work to let you know I am thinking of you. Then I text you when you will be just arriving to let you know I am thinking about what we did last night. I add an emoji of a wink. I try to call you at the time you will be heading off on break, but you do not pick up. So I try again ten minutes later. And again five minutes after that.

Still at home, I get ready for work. I take a long shower and dress with care. I briefly consider moving my things back from the box room to the bedroom. Then I think about what Julie might say if she was here and decide to wait until you suggest it yourself. I think Julie would be pleased.

When I still haven't heard from you by

lunchtime, when I am due to leave, I start to get annoyed. I know that you might be confused, but what would a call cost you? A text, even? I phone you again as I am walking to the car. And again after I drop off my first fare.

I do an airport run to Luton. The client in the back of my cab is chatty and, normally, I am OK with that, but today I find it hard to engage. When we get stuck in traffic outside the terminal, I have to close my eyes and count to ten so I don't slam my fists against the steering wheel.

It is after four when my phone pings to show a text message from you. I am driving around Hanger Lane in West London. When I glance across and see your name on the screen, it is like someone opening a valve inside me and letting out tension. I don't look at the text while I am driving, but knowing it is there gives me a warm glow inside.

I drop off my fare in Wembley and put my hazard lights on while I read your text. I am hoping you will tell me you have been to Tesco on your way home to pick up something nice for dinner. A celebration of our new start. When I read your text I have to read it again straight away because I am so sure I have read it wrong.

I am sorry, you say. *Last night was a mistake.*

I have not changed my mind. We are not getting back together. Please forget it happened.

The words jump out at me. *Sorry. Mistake. Forget.* Each one is a punch to my stomach. For a moment I think I will be sick, and I open the car window so I can breathe in the fresh air.

I have to make a pick-up in Brent Cross so I start driving. A knot of hatred forms in my gut as big as a fist.

Chapter Nine

'You don't need to tell me. I know I'm an idiot.'

Kate is stirring chilli with one hand, and her phone is tucked between her ear and her shoulder so Mel's voice sounds like it is coming from far away.

'What the hell got into you?' Mel is saying.

'I don't know. It was a mixture of talking about how things used to be and feeling at a low point and drinking bucket-loads of wine. We got carried away. That's all. And then, of course, he thought that meant we were back on again. He's been calling and texting the entire day.'

'And what about Tom?' Mel wants to know.

Kate groans.

'He doesn't know. He must never know. The thing with Jack last night just made me even more sure that Tom is the one I want to be with.'

After the call ends, Kate puts the lid on the chilli and sits down heavily at the kitchen table. How can she have been so stupid? Jack was just getting used to the idea of them being apart, and now she has gone and confused everything. She sent the text more than three hours ago and still he has not replied.

She knows how hurt he will be. And how angry.

She is dreading Amy and Ben coming down for dinner, because she knows they will ask her questions about their dad. Jack is not the only one who will be hurt and confused by what happened last night.

'But I thought that meant you and Dad were back together,' Amy says, as Kate dishes out the chilli and tries to explain.

Her eyes fill with tears, reminding Kate again just how young she still is.

'I'm sorry, baby,' says Kate, making her way around the table to give Amy a hug. 'Marriage is complicated.'

'Yeah, well, I'm glad you're not getting back with him,' says Ben. 'I love him, because he's my dad, but I hate his moods. He scares me sometimes.'

Kate is surprised. She has never heard Ben talk like this about Jack. She pushes her food around her plate but cannot eat.

After dinner the kids go back to their rooms and Kate flops down in front of the television.

There is a nature programme on that she usually enjoys, but she cannot focus on it. Instead, she thinks about Jack and what he will do now. She hopes that he will accept what she has said. Maybe he is even thinking the same thing. That it was a mistake.

But, deep down, she knows he isn't.

The house feels weird. As if it is holding its breath. She pictures little particles of tension hanging in the air like specks of dust. Since last night something has been niggling at her, but she still cannot work out what it is.

She sends a text to Tom to tell him she is thinking about him.

Still no word from Jack.

In the middle of the night Kate hears Amy shouting.

'I heard those noises from the roof again, Mum,' she says when Kate goes into her room.

Kate listens but doesn't hear anything.

'It's just squirrels, like I told you,' she tells Amy.

But when she gets back into her own bed she lies awake, unable to sleep. And when she does finally drop off, just as the dawn light is creeping in around the blackout curtains, she dreams there's a monster standing by her bed, breathing in the dark.

Chapter Ten

JACK: Monday afternoon,
fifteen days after the split

You have a lover.

I feel sick.

I call Lynne at the cab office and tell her I'm not well and can't work. She sounds surprised. 'This is the first time in fifteen years you have called in sick,' she says.

'First time for everything,' I say, and pretend to laugh.

Afterwards, I put my head in my hands and rock backwards and forwards. I try to stop the movies in my mind, but I can't. You with him. Doing what we did last Thursday night.

He came to the door early this morning before you left for work. You didn't let him in, but I got a good look. What can you see in him? He is younger than me, that's true, but he is thin and pale and his hair needs a cut. I could see right away he hasn't set foot in a gym. I could knock him over just by blowing on him.

46

He held up a greasy brown paper bag. 'I come bearing gifts,' he said.

Bearing gifts? This is the man you think is better than me?

You told him he shouldn't have come. Said the kids were in the house. You tried to make your voice stern, but you turned your face to the side and I saw you hiding a smile. Then you looked behind to make sure no one was there and you kissed him. Right there on my doorstep. I saw his hand go down to your bum and I thought I would vomit. Felt the bile rising in my throat. But I swallowed it down.

'Go. GO!' you said to him, and pushed him away. But it was in that playful kind of way that shows you don't really mean it.

He walked away backwards, holding up his hands as if in surrender.

He mouthed, 'Later,' and licked his lips.

I want to kill him.

'Who was that?' asked Amy, coming into the hallway just as you shut the door.

'Only Karen, from across the road,' you said. 'She brought us some croissants.'

When did you get so good at lying?

All day I have sat without moving while the images played out in my mind. His hand on your bum. Your smirking face. His tongue coming out to lick his lips.

What have you done?

Don't you remember the vows you made to me?

It has got dark while I have been sitting here. And my stomach is groaning for lack of food. My right calf has cramp because I haven't moved in so long. But I hardly notice the pain in my leg because the pain in my head is so strong.

At around five forty-five you come back home. The first thing you do is go around turning on the lights. You look nervous.

Have I scared you? Good.

You take out your phone, and for a moment I think you are calling *him* and feel the acid rush of anger in my veins. But then you say, 'Mel. You got a minute?'

You tell her that you haven't slept. You say you feel awful. But then a smile creeps across your face and you say, 'Tom was here this morning.' And I realize that she knows. Mel. That bitch knows you have a lover. And she's clearly OK with that.

'No,' you say to her. 'It isn't because he found out about Jack. Thank God. I still can't believe I did that. I've felt grubby ever since.'

And now it does come. A string of yellow bile

that goes straight on to the floor. Grubby. I'm her husband, and she feels grubby after being with me. It is beyond belief.

'I *am* being careful,' she says into the phone. 'You don't need to remind me what he's like. I was married to him for sixteen years.'

Now Mel says something else. And you sigh. 'I don't know which friend he's staying with,' you say. 'All I know is all his stuff is still here in the box room. I can't wait for it to go.'

You are sitting at the kitchen table while you say all this. And after the call has finished you put your phone down next to you and stare into space.

And I watch you. From my secret hide-out in the attic.

But you have no idea.

There's a drop of bile on the screen, and I wipe it away with the sleeve of my jumper. It is cold up here so I am wearing two jumpers, one over the other. After two weeks in the attic I am used to it. But the first night I spent up here I thought I might die. I wondered how long my body would lie up here before the smell gave it away.

Sometimes, when I think properly about where I am and how far things have gone, I feel like I can't breathe. Hiding, like a rat, in the attic of my own home. Only coming out when everyone else is out or asleep. Stealing food from my own fridge in my own kitchen.

It started after you told me you wanted a divorce. After that scene in the kitchen when I sat and looked at you, and waited for you to say you were joking but you never did.

Were you sleeping with him then? I wonder. Croissant Man? *Tom?* Even while you said all those things to me that seemed to come straight from a bad film script.

It's not you, it's me.

I love you, but I'm not in love with you.

I just need space.

Kids adapt.

Did you meet up with him afterwards and have a bloody good laugh about it? While he touched you in all your secret places that are mine to know?

I bet you laid it on thick. About how your husband lost it when you told him you didn't want to be with him any more. Well, who wouldn't? Out of the blue like that. *I want a divorce.*

I'm not proud of what I did. Of losing control. I know you were fond of that dinner set from your mother. I shouldn't have smashed it up, or punched a hole through the kitchen door after you tried to shut me out. But I never laid a hand on you. Did I? You never gave me credit for that. And afterwards, when I'd cooled off, I came home and helped you clear up, didn't I?

And then I knelt on the floor amidst the piles of china and glass and I begged you to change your mind. I wept. Do you remember? A grown man. On his knees. Crying. I said I'd do anything. Anything at all. How you must have laughed.

And when you said, again, that you needed space, I offered to move my stuff into the box room. Said I would go and stay with a friend. Anything so long as you agreed to think about it, agreed it wasn't yet over.

I thought it was a phase. PMT, maybe. And that, when you'd made your point, we'd go back to normal. I thought you just needed time.

But I'm not an idiot. I wasn't about to move out of the home I pay for, leaving you free to do God knows what.

The next day, when you were out at work and the kids were at school, I set it all up. Tiny spy camera recorders hidden in fake smoke alarms in the living room and the kitchen and the hall. I got them on Amazon. Next-day delivery. They look just like a real smoke alarm. You never noticed the difference. They detect movement.

So they start recording whenever someone comes into the room, and it gets transmitted via the Wi-Fi straight to my phone.

So clever what they can do these days.

Then I set up home in the attic. I tried to make it cosy. Sleeping bag. Clothes. Food and water. A Thermos. A bucket for when I can't get to the toilet. It's not as bad as it could be. Two years ago, when we almost got the loft converted, we had the floor boarded and the sloping walls plastered, but then we decided it wasn't high enough. Even at its highest point, I can't stand up without hunching right over. And though the kids would have been all right back then, we knew they would soon be too tall. So we never bothered with the windows. Just carried on using it to store junk.

When the heating is on, it gets so hot and airless up here that it is hard to breathe. But other times, when it is cold outside, there's a chill that soaks into my bones.

The hatch to the attic is above the landing. There's one of those ladders you hook down with a pole which we've always kept just inside the airing cupboard. When I am coming up here, I always have to make sure I put the pole back in the airing cupboard before pulling the ladder up behind me. When I get down I don't bother with the ladder at all. I just jump. Then close the hatch with the pole.

With a camera in the hallway, I know when everyone has left the house and it's safe to come down. I'm always careful. A few pieces of ham. A banana. When I use the shower, I dry my feet thoroughly so I don't leave footprints on the mat.

I have bottled water up here and boxes of crisps and biscuits. I don't go hungry.

You didn't try too hard to find out which friend I was staying with. Too happy to be rid of me, I expect.

But the thing is, it was supposed to be temporary. Just until you had come to your senses and asked me to come back. Which I knew you would. You are not a woman who likes to be alone.

I thought that, once you'd seen how good I was being about everything, you would change your mind. You asked for space, so I gave it to you. I kept going to see the counsellor, even though she says things like, 'Let's imagine what a divorce might look like.' I did all that because I thought you would change your mind and beg me to come home. I thought that maybe, one day, I might even tell you about all this. Tell you about the sleeping bag in the attic, the hours of watching you on my phone.

You would think it was romantic. The things I did for love of you.

But I didn't know you were fucking someone else.

That changes things. That changes *everything*.

Chapter Eleven

'You don't look well at all,' says Mel.

Though Kate is used to her best friend's bluntness, it still stings. She feels bad enough already, without knowing that her misery is reflected in her face.

'Yeah, well. Breaking up is bloody hard to do. Hey, I should write a song about that.' Kate is trying to sound jokey, but nothing feels funny at the moment.

They are sitting in the living room on opposite ends of the sofa. Mel is peering at her intently and Kate knows she can see right through her. They've known each other since they were fifteen and there is nothing she can hide from Mel. Mel was even there the first night she met Jack.

'I warned you about him,' Mel says now, as if she has read Kate's mind.

Kate sighs. It's true. When they walked into that pub after the gym, she hadn't even noticed

55

Jack until Mel said, 'Jesus, could that bloke over there stare any harder, do you think? He's freaking me out.'

Then she'd looked over, straight into his piercing blue eyes, and it had been like being tasered or something. She'd said that to him once, and he'd laughed and said, 'My cunning plan worked, then? To shoot an invisible dart into you with an invisible wire attached so you could never get away?'

When she had first started seeing him, he showered her with gifts and flowers and texts. Mel had told her it was over the top, but Kate didn't agree. She was flattered by him wanting to be with her all the time. 'He can't bear to be without me,' she told Mel proudly. 'He says I am all he thinks about.'

Who would have thought that would come to feel like a huge boulder tied around her neck?

Mel is stroking Sid. The cat is lying on its back on the sofa in between them with its legs stretched out above its head. He looks so content and comfortable, Kate is almost jealous.

'I would be okay if I could just sleep,' Kate says. 'I try to go to bed early, but I lie there in the dark for hour after hour with my heart racing.'

'You're going to make yourself ill,' says Mel. 'I can tell you're not eating properly. You've lost a ton of weight, and you didn't have any to lose. Not like me.'

She looks down at her shirt, which is stretched tight over her stomach, and sighs. Then she leans over and plucks out a fun-sized Mars bar from the open packet on the coffee table.

'In for a penny,' she says.

'I'm going to go away for a couple of weeks,' Kate says. 'When the kids break up for Easter. Take them to my parents in Cornwall. Get some sleep. All that sea air.'

'Good idea,' says Mel. 'Clear your head.'

'I need to,' says Kate. 'I still can't believe I was that stupid.'

Kate is talking about sleeping with Jack on Thursday night.

'At least tell me the sex was good,' says Mel.

Kate makes a face like she has swallowed a piece of lemon.

'I knew it was a mistake as soon as we'd gone to bed, but I was drunk and it seemed like the easiest thing was to go through the motions,' she says. 'To be honest, Mel, he made my skin crawl.'

'Not like gorgeous Tom, then?' says Mel, smiling, and revealing teeth still stained brown with chocolate.

Kate feels her cheeks grow hot.

'Let's change the subject.'

Mel laughs. 'Spoilsport,' she says.

Then she grows serious. 'I'm so happy you've finally got away from Jack,' she says. 'All these years, I've been begging you to leave him. And what a relief that he seems to be taking it so calmly. Do you know, I thought you might never get rid of him?'

Chapter Twelve

JACK: Monday evening,
fifteen days after the split

It is like there is a red veil over my eyes turning everything the colour of blood.

I shut them tight, but now all I can hear is the whooshing of my own blood in my ears and, above that, the echo of Mel's words.

All these years, I've been begging you to leave him.
I thought you might never get rid of him.

I picture Mel's brown-stained teeth, as she laughed, after you said that thing about me making your skin crawl. Hatred swims through my veins until I am alive with it.

I watch you get up, watch Mel pop an extra chocolate bar in her bag when you are not looking. Watch you walk her to the front door and give her a hug. She is at least six inches shorter than you, so you get a mouthful of frizzy blonde hair.

After she's gone, you head to the kitchen and play George Michael very loudly. I shouldn't risk coming out. Not when Ben and Amy are in their bedrooms and I'll have to go right past their doors. But they'll both have their headphones in. And if I sit up here much longer I think I might explode.

I open the hatch carefully and listen. Nothing. I lower myself down on to the carpet below. I've taken off my shoes and tied them around my neck by their laces so I don't make a sound. I consider leaving the hatch open. Ben and Amy are so wrapped up in themselves, what are the chances of them looking up and noticing? But in the end, I decide I'm taking enough risks already. I get the stick from the airing cupboard and hook the hatch closed.

I pad downstairs in my socks. I can hear George Michael blasting from the kitchen, but I still wait until I am outside the front door before putting my shoes on.

I know exactly which way Mel will have gone. I know exactly which bus she needs to get to go home. It's raining, and my hair is plastered to my head, but I don't care. It feels good to be out of the attic.

But still hatred is pumping through my body, making its way into every cell, every hair follicle. I am pulsing with it.

There is a crowd at the bus stop. It happens. The buses are supposed to come every ten minutes but, usually, it's more like twenty. I spot Mel straight away. That frizz of hair. Do you remember that Christmas when your boss gave you a hamper of fancy food packed with shredded paper straw? I put a load of it on my head and asked you to guess who I was. You were giggling like mad, though you pretended to tell me off.

And now you're taking her side against me?

Mel never liked me. She was jealous. That was the problem. The sourness came off her in waves, like stale sweat.

She never missed an opportunity to put me down. After she found out I left school at sixteen, she liked to call me your bit of rough. She would spell out long words on the menu if we went out to eat. 'It's only a bit of fun,' you always said. 'She's just having a joke with you.'

The crowd at the bus stop surges forward. I peer down the street through the rain, which is now coming down in sheets. The bus is approaching, and already it is clear there are people standing up inside. The people at the bus stop mutter loudly. If the bus is too full already, they won't all get on. They start pushing, trying to get to the front. I can see Mel standing by the kerb, her hair soaking, determined not to get left behind.

It is all too easy.

As the bus draws near, there is another surge, with people pressing each other to get to the doors. I shove my way through until there is just one person between me and Mel. People are getting angry. Someone shouts at someone else to the side of me. No one notices when I reach my arm around the person in front so that the flat of my hand is against Mel's back. I give a short, hard push, just as the bus pulls in.

There is a screech of brakes. Somebody screams.

In the confusion, I melt back into the crowd and slip quietly away.

Chapter Thirteen

'Sit down. Let me get that for you.'

Kate jumps up to snatch the kettle out of Mel's hand.

Mel doesn't bother to protest.

'Thanks,' she says, shuffling back to her chair, where she drops down with a sigh.

'They said those would get easier in time, but I still can't get the hang of them.' She is pointing to the crutches which lean up against the table in her cosy kitchen.

It is three days after the accident and Mel is trying to put on a brave face, but Kate can see how shaken she still is. They have known each other too long to hide things from each other.

'You still having flashbacks?' she asks.

Mel nods. 'Every time I close my eyes I'm back there at the bus stop. Feeling myself falling. Hearing the screech of the brakes. You know, if that driver had been going any faster, I'd be dead. That's what the police said. He wouldn't have been able to stop in time and I'd have gone under the wheels.'

As it was, the bus had almost stopped by the time it hit her. Even so, she was still thrown several feet, landing with her right leg bent underneath her.

'I've been saying for ages that it's an accident waiting to happen, that bus stop,' says Kate. 'The pavement is way too narrow. And when there's a gap between buses, it gets really crowded. Especially at rush hour.'

'That's what the policeman said. He said you couldn't blame the people behind me because they were also being pushed. There's going to be an official investigation. To stop it happening to some other poor bugger.'

'But are you OK? You still don't seem to be back to your old self.'

'I'll live. And what about you, Kate? You haven't ended up back in bed with Jack again, I hope.'

'No way. That was a one-off.'

'And Tom?'

Kate shakes her head. 'To be honest, Mel, your accident shook me up so much I haven't wanted to do anything except stay home and cuddle the kids. I'm still not sleeping well. My nerves are on edge. And the bloody squirrels in the roof don't help much. As soon as I get paid, I'm going to get those sorted out. Do you know, I can't wait for term to be over so I can get away with Ben and Amy and relax properly.'

She looks at her phone.

'Shit. I have to go. I'm meeting Jack at the counsellor's in twenty minutes.'

'I don't know why you still bother going to see her. It's over, isn't it? What's the point?'

'Jack is still Ben and Amy's dad. It's important to try to get on with him. And I don't want to make an enemy of him. You know how he can be. There's still so much to sort out. Like where he's going to live. He can't go on kipping at his mate's for ever, but he goes crazy if I suggest he rents a room in a flat. I'm scared he's going to try to force me to sell the house.'

'He can't do that. Not if you have custody of the kids.'

'I wouldn't put it past him to go for custody himself. He keeps threatening to.'

'They'd laugh him out of the court room,' says Mel. 'He has never been hands-on with them. Not even when they were young. He wouldn't recognize a nappy if you slapped him around the face with one.'

'Still, I've got to keep on his good side, if I can. For the kids' sake.'

As she makes her way to Julie's house, Kate can't shake off a feeling of dread. What happened to Mel has upset her more than she has let on. What if she had died? The thing is, you never know, do you, when the end might come? It is so important to do the right thing. Make the right choices.

She is late getting to Julie's and Jack is already there, with a face like thunder. She hasn't even sat down before he starts. On and on about her having a lover. Why is he so fixated on that? He can't possibly know about Tom. She has been so careful.

'You really need to let this go. It is holding you back,' Julie tells Jack. Her voice is gentle, but Kate feels Jack grow tense on the sofa beside her.

Afterwards, she will wonder what made her speak out. Perhaps it is to do with Mel and doing the right thing while there is still time. Or perhaps she just feels sorry for Jack, who is still her husband, after all.

'Jack is right. Well, almost right,' she says to Julie. 'There was another man who paid me attention, and I was tempted. But I didn't do it.'

'Oh,' says Julie, giving her a cross-eyed stare. 'So it wasn't all in Jack's head?'

'No. Well, not *all* of it,' says Kate, wishing now

that she had never said anything. 'Like I said, nothing happened.'

'And it's over now?'

'Yes,' says Kate firmly.

To her left, she hears Jack let out a deep breath.

'You know coming to see me only works if you are willing to be completely honest, Kate,' says Julie. 'Otherwise, it's a waste of all our time.'

It is too much for Kate. The worry about Mel, the fights with Jack and now the counsellor telling her off. She bursts into tears.

'I'm sorry,' she says, wiping her eyes with a tissue from the box on the table in front of her. 'My best friend has been in an accident, so I am very emotional at the moment.'

'I am so sorry to hear that,' says Julie.

'Me, too,' says Jack. He reaches out and puts his hand on hers. 'Mel and I might not see eye to eye on things, but I was really shocked when Amy told me what happened.'

After the counselling, Kate is still upset and Jack insists on driving her home.

'I meant what I said in there,' he says when they are in the car. 'I'm glad Mel is OK.'

Kate feels something inside her give way. She has been too hard on Jack. He is still the man she fell in love with. Still soft when it comes to her. When they pull up outside the house, she lets him put his arms around her. She leans her head against his chest.

'Did you mean it about that bloke?' he whispers. 'That it's over?'

She nods, her cheek brushing against his jumper.

And, just for that moment, it is true.

Chapter Fourteen

JACK: Friday night,
nineteen days after the split

It takes me ages to warm up. After I dropped you off, I had to sit in the car for hours waiting for you all to go to sleep before I could let myself into the house and up to the attic without being seen.

It makes me nervous coming in and out while there are people in the house, especially after you said you aren't sleeping well. But I've done it so many times that it is easy now I know exactly which stairs are noisiest, which bit of the landing carpet hides the creaking floorboard.

Now, sitting here wearing two hoodies and the sleeping bag, I keep going over and over what happened today. Are you telling the truth? Is there really no more Tom, with his bag of greasy pastries and his too-long hair? Are you coming back to me?

Hope fizzes and pops in my bloodstream.

I look around the attic. Though the walls and ceiling are plastered and the floor is solid, there are cobwebs in the corners and piles of stuff which I have shoved to one end. Suitcases. Boxes of old kids' toys and clothes. I don't know how many times I begged you to get rid of them.

'I'm saving these for when Amy and Ben have kids of their own,' you always said.

No point trying to tell you that this stuff will seem like it's from the Dark Ages by then.

I've hated being up here. Listening to the noise of bird claws scratching around above my head. Feeling cold, but at the same time suffocating. Yet, now that it looks as if I will soon be moving back downstairs, I find myself feeling almost fond of the place. It has served me well. How many other men in my position have been able to stay so close to their families? Keeping watch on everything they do?

I have a seven-hour shift the day after counselling. Normally, I have my phone on silent while I'm driving, but today I am waiting for you to call me, so I leave the sound on. So I don't miss it.

You don't call.

At lunchtime I call in for a sandwich in the usual cafe and send you a text. *Thinking about you.* It's short and not too needy. But you don't reply.

As it's Friday, it is my evening with Ben and

Amy. Your idea is that, eventually, I will have them to stay with me every other weekend. But, until I get a place of my own, I am to take them out every other Friday night. I have pretended to go along with it. But it is never going to happen. See my kids just every other weekend? No way.

We go for pizza. They are pleased to see me at first, but soon they get bored. Ben is missing a night out with his mates. And Amy would rather be home watching Netflix and messaging her friends.

'You have to stop quizzing us about Mum the whole time,' she says, when I ask a perfectly harmless question. 'Just face it. It's finished.'

'Or maybe not,' I say. And smile so they don't know if I'm joking.

I'm not joking.

I have my phone in my pocket set to vibrate so I will know the second you get in touch. You don't get in touch. I keep remembering how you leaned into me in the car, wanting me to hold you. Surely it is only a matter of time until you call?

When I go to the loo I check my phone to make sure it is working.

I try to persuade the kids to stay out after dinner. We could go to the cinema, I suggest. I know I will have to stay out until late, waiting for everyone to go to bed so that I can sneak into the loft. The empty hours stretch ahead of me.

But Amy and Ben want to go home. Back to their laptops and their friends. When I drop them off, the house is in darkness.

'Mum gone out then?' I ask.

They shrug.

'The thing is,' says Ben, 'it's not really your business any more.'

He doesn't say it to be unkind. It is just a statement of fact. Even so, I feel a surge of red-hot rage and have to curl my fingers up into fists and count to ten in my head.

I think about telling them that you have changed your mind. That things will soon be back to normal. But there is something about the dark rooms and not knowing where you are, or what you are doing, or who you are doing it with, that stops me.

I park at the end of the road, where I can watch the house. It is after midnight when you arrive home in a taxi and nearly 2 a.m. before I dare let myself in. I am so tired, but I am wide awake. It feels as if there are lines of ants crawling through my veins. At least tomorrow is Saturday, so I can stay up here in the attic all day looking at you.

Lying in my sleeping bag on the loft floor, I turn on my phone and flick through all the camera views – living room, kitchen, hallway – but all are dark and still.

I wish I had put a smoke alarm in the bedroom so I could watch you sleep.

Chapter Fifteen

KATE: Saturday morning,
twenty days after the split

'Did you have a good time with Dad?'

Amy shrugs, her mouth full of Cheerios.

'It was OK, I suppose,' she says.

'Please tell me we don't have to do that every Friday night,' Ben says, glaring at her over his steaming tea. 'I missed a really good night out.'

'Just till things get sorted,' Kate says. 'I promise.'

The kids both tell her they will be out this evening. To make up for missing out the night before. Amy is on a sleepover with her best friend and Ben is going to a party. 'We're all crashing at Jake's afterwards,' he tells her. 'Safer than coming home alone,' he adds, when she tries to protest.

So now she has the house to herself for a whole night.

After the kids have gone back upstairs, Kate puts on the radio while she cleans up the kitchen.

She feels embarrassed now that she fell apart

in counselling the evening before last. She was with Mel last night, and her friend is so much better. Back to her old self. She wishes she hadn't let Jack drive her home, or put his arms around her. She does not want to give him false hope. There is something strange about the way he is handling everything. He is too calm. Something bothers her about him, but she cannot work out what it is. And she regrets telling him about Tom. She was at such a low point. That's why she admitted there had been someone else interested, and why she lied about it being over.

It is not over.

Kate decides she will invite Tom over later. It is too good a chance to pass up. Tom lives in a two-bedroomed flat that he shares with a couple who rarely go out. Kate never quite relaxes when she goes round there. This is a chance for them to be on their own for once.

Also, though she does not like to admit it, she will be glad not to be alone in the house. Since Jack left, everything has felt strange. The noises at night. The sense of things being disturbed. Food going missing. Someone in her bed. It must be Amy or Ben, of course, although they deny it. But still, it makes her feel on edge.

After Amy and Ben go out, she spends a long time getting ready. A half-an-hour soak in the bath. Home-waxing her legs with those strips that make her yelp with pain. Plucking her eyebrows.

She dresses with care. A pale blue silk top with tight denim jeans and high-heeled shoes. Best underwear. She twists her hair back and secures it with a clip. Jack always used to like her to leave it long and loose. Tom is different.

When Tom arrives, he can tell how nervous she is. As soon as the front door closes behind him, he takes her in his arms and kisses her deeply in the hallway.

'Better now?' he asks, when they pull apart.

She nods.

He has brought a bottle of champagne and they go into the kitchen to fetch glasses. She is making a beef stew with a red wine sauce. When she gets up to stir it, he pulls her down on to his lap and they kiss again. By the time they finish their second glasses of champagne, they have lost all interest in food. Instead, they go upstairs to the bedroom.

For the next hour or so, Kate is lost in what she and Tom are doing. It is only when she gets up, naked, to go to the bathroom that she gets that strange, prickling feeling again. As if the house itself is angry with her.

After a while, they are hungry and they go

downstairs to eat. Kate realizes how much she loves having Tom there in her kitchen. He is so full of compliments. About her. About her cooking. Her home.

'You are an amazing woman,' he tells her. After all those years with Jack pointing out her faults, she feels a warm glow of pride.

They go into the living room and cuddle up together on the sofa. Tom tells her he is DJ'ing tomorrow lunchtime in a chill-out bar in town. He does it for fun, he says. He asks her if she will come along, and she is tempted but says she had better not. She is taking Amy and Ben to her parents' house in Cornwall on Monday and needs to get things ready.

Tom does not stay the night. Just in case the kids come back early. But it is nearly 3 a.m. by the time he tears himself away. Yet still he cannot bring himself to leave.

'I need to tell you something,' he says, standing on the doorstep. 'I think I am falling in love with you.'

Kate's heart expands in her chest until she feels it might burst.

'Me, too,' she says.

Afterwards, she lies in her bed, reliving the evening, remembering the things they said and did. How it all felt.

She knows she needs to sleep, but the anxiety is back, prickling at her skin like an ice-cold needle. She thinks she can hear the squirrels scratching above Amy's room. Even when she does finally drop off, her sleep is disturbed.

She dreams she hears a man crying as if his heart would break.

Chapter Sixteen

JACK: Sunday morning,
twenty-one days after the split

How could you? How could you? How could you?
I am walking around the early-morning streets, and the words are stuck in my head like an annoying tune that I can't shake off.
How could you?
With him?
I have no idea how long I've been walking. After he left I was in shock. I sat there in the loft, shaking and crying. The images played out in my head as if they were on a loop. I shouldn't have watched. But I couldn't look away. My wife. My Kate. You. With *him.*
Twice, I was sick in the bucket in the corner. The smell was disgusting. In the end I had to creep down from the loft and come outside to gulp down lungfuls of fresh air. Since then I've been walking. While the sky turned pink and then orange and now the deep navy blue of spilled ink.
I cannot believe I have been so stupid. I let you

lie to me. I let you tell me it was over. Whatever 'it' might be. You have made a fool of me. The two of you. Laughing at me.

You will both pay.

This is my second night without sleep. My feet are moving, one in front of the other, but I do not know how. I am like a robot. Except robots don't feel pain.

How could you?

It is too risky now to go back into the house, so I must stay outside, walking to keep warm. While you are cosy in our bed. The bed where you had sex with another man. On sheets we bought together in the Boxing Day sale.

Rage is a white-hot blade, twisting in my gut.

At ten o'clock I go back to the house. I cannot keep away.

I ring on the bell.

'Oh,' you say.

I force my mouth into a smile.

'Just thought I would pop by and see how you all are,' I say. 'You never replied to my text. I wanted to make sure you were all right.'

'I'm fine,' you say. 'I've just been busy.'

That's when I lose it.

'I'll bet you've been busy,' I say. 'Busy shagging *him. Croissant Man.* After everything you said about it being over.'

Your face turns the colour the sun was a few hours ago. The colour of a blood orange.

'It is over,' you lie. Then: 'Have you been spying on me?'

I can see your mind racing. You are wondering how much I know. And how I know it. I see your eyes flick across the street, wondering where I could have hidden myself to keep watch on the house.

'I don't need to spy. I can smell him on you.'

You slam the door in my face. I ring a few more times. I think about using my key but don't want to risk you taking it off me.

Finally, I walk away. There's a movement at the upstairs window and I know you've been watching me, waiting for me to leave.

I almost laugh out loud, imagining your relief, thinking you have got rid of me. I will be back. Don't you worry. But there's something I need to do first.

I find the bar without a problem. I remember him telling you it was called The First Floor when he was trying to get you to come along.

I remember everything.

It's not the kind of place I normally go. There are sofas and armchairs and little low tables with board games on them. Board games, for fuck's sake.

They only sell bottled beer, and when I hand the barman a fiver he only gives me fifty pence change.

I recognize Tom straight away. That stupid hair that he has to keep flicking out of his eyes. Playing boring music that makes you want to slit your wrists. He doesn't know who I am, of course, so I get to stare at him to my heart's content.

Every now and then his eyes dart over my way. As if he senses me looking.

How could you?

With him?

By the time he finishes his set, there are six empty bottles of beer on the table in front of me. But my mind feels razor sharp.

I have the car parked outside, but *he* takes off on foot. I follow him. Ten minutes. Fifteen. As long as it takes. It is getting dark now, and I stay a long way behind him. I keep close to the wall, ready to duck into doorways, but still he looks over his shoulder two or three times, as if he can feel me watching him.

Finally, he turns into a gate that leads to a tall semi-detached house. There are three bells by the front door, which means three flats in the building. I watch as a light goes on in the ground floor window, then I make my way around the side of the house. There is a gate, which is locked, but it is easy to put a foot up on the heavy metal bolt, and hatred carries me right over the top.

I have no plan of what I am going to do. But I know something will come up. The garden is small and overgrown. I hide myself behind a bush near the back and wait.

After forty-five minutes, the back door opens and *he* appears. He lights up a cigarette and stands in the doorway, inhaling deeply.

At one point his phone makes a sound and he takes it out of his pocket. The screen is lit up and bathes the bottom half of his face in a silver glow, as he reads whatever is written.

I know it is a text from you. And now he smiles, a secret smile that makes me want to smash his face until there is nothing left of it.

He goes back inside.

He doesn't lock the door.

Chapter Seventeen

KATE: Sunday evening,
twenty-one days after the split

Tom is dead.

No matter how many times she tells herself that fact, she still cannot take it in.

A fire. He fell asleep in the chair in the living room, smoking a cigarette. The chair caught fire. And then the curtains. His flatmates were away for the weekend so the fire had taken hold before anyone noticed. Tom was dragged out of his flat by an upstairs neighbour but died in the ambulance due to inhaling smoke.

A bottle of whisky was found at the scene, and witnesses from The First Floor bar said he'd been drinking throughout the afternoon.

According to the policeman who came round to see her, a friend said Tom had boasted of having hardly any sleep the night before. He had winked when he said it.

The policeman was only interviewing Kate because they were putting together a picture of his movements over the weekend before he died.

'Could it have been arson?' Kate asked, when she could finally speak, after she had run to the sink and retched until her stomach was sore.

'We're not looking for anyone else at this stage,' the policeman said.

He was a young man with an Adam's apple that looked as if he had a golf ball lodged in his throat. Kate focused on that golf ball to ward off another wave of nausea.

Now the policeman has gone and she is sitting in the kitchen with her head in her hands. Her thoughts are going round and round in her head like in a washing machine.

For the first hour or so after the policeman left, all she could think of was Tom, and the look in his green eyes when he told her he was falling in love with her.

But now her thoughts have moved to Jack. How his mouth had twisted up when he'd said, 'I can smell him on you.' The hatred coming off him in waves.

It's just coincidence, she tells herself. *Jack would not do that.* Then she remembers all the times when her husband had lost control. The times when he had thrown things and broken things and had looked at her as if he wanted to kill her. And she shivers.

She thinks back to the last time she saw Jack.

Standing on her doorstep. What was it he had called Tom? Croissant Man? He must have been watching when Tom arrived at the door with a brown paper bag. But something doesn't add up.

She can still picture Tom standing there. Holding up the bag. How did Jack know there were croissants in there?

There is a cold feeling in the pit of her stomach, as if she has swallowed a lump of ice. She thinks of the food going missing from the fridge. The vodka replaced by water. The rumpled bed. The science text book picked up from the living-room floor while she was out at work. There is something else that has been niggling at her, too. Something he said in counselling. She forces herself to concentrate. And now she remembers. When Julie had got them to say things they liked about each other. He'd said she used to be a good mum. Patient. Not shouting at them. *Not like now, with the bed and the vodka.* That's what he'd said.

But how had he known that she'd argued with Amy about being in her bedroom, and with Ben about replacing her vodka with water?

The kids must have told him, she tells herself. But she knows it isn't true. Amy and Ben wouldn't tell tales on her to Jack.

The cold feeling spreads from her stomach to

her chest, freezing the blood around her heart.

He has been in the house, watching her.

She sits upright. Her eyes dart around the room. How is he doing it? Her eye is caught by a tiny prick of red light that seems to be coming from inside the smoke detector. Normally, she doesn't pay any attention to the white discs on the ceiling, but now she pauses. If there is a light, shouldn't it be green?

Her heart is thudding in her ribcage as she drags a chair underneath the smoke alarm and reaches up to twist off the cover, as she has done before when the battery needed changing.

There is no battery inside. Just a lot of coloured wires. And a memory card and a tiny microphone and a camera.

For a moment, the room sways and she thinks she will faint. She drops down on to the chair and sits with her head between her knees.

Then something else occurs to her.

The noises in the roof.

No, she says to herself. *He wouldn't.*

But even as she is thinking it, she is moving out of the kitchen and up the stairs, and taking the pole that they keep in the airing cupboard. She is hooking it over the loop on the hatch. And tugging it open. And now she is reaching up to unhook the ladder with the pole, and she is pulling it down and climbing up the steps, even though she doesn't like going up in the loft. And . . . *oh!*

A sleeping bag, unrolled on the bare floor. Packets of food and plastic water bottles piled in one corner. A bad-smelling bucket in another corner.

He has been living here. Watching her through the cameras downstairs.

Now she remembers about Tom coming to the house. She scrambles down the stairs and runs to the bedroom, almost collapsing with relief when she sees there is no smoke alarm on the ceiling.

But still she feels violated.

He watched her. He watched Tom. He watched them together in the hall and the living room and the kitchen.

And then he did something to Tom. She is sure of it.

She sinks to the floor and lies there for a very long time.

Chapter Eighteen

JACK: Monday morning,
twenty-two days after the split

Safely back in the loft, I cannot believe I have got away with it.

I pick up my phone from the top of the sleeping bag next to me. I go to the website of the local paper and read the headline for the hundredth time, even though I know it off by heart.

FIRE THAT KILLED LOCAL MAN STARTED FROM LIT CIGARETTE

I am in the clear.

Twenty hours on, and my hands have almost stopped shaking.

Still holding my phone, I flick through all the cameras, half expecting to see police coming through the front door and up the stairs, but there is nothing. You are all in the kitchen. You are taking the kids to your parents later, and Amy and Ben are already arguing about who will have the front seat in the car. You are pale and there are dark rings around your eyes. But you tell them to shush and make themselves sandwiches, as if this is a normal day.

I could cry from relief.

I hadn't planned to kill him. It was a split-second thing. When I crept in through the unlocked back door, I was only going to scare him. But then I saw he'd fallen asleep in the chair in the living room. With a half-empty bottle of whisky in front of him. I remembered what he was doing the night before with you to make him so tired, and a red mist came down.

There was only one smoke alarm downstairs, in the kitchen, so I took the battery out of that and left it hanging open, as if someone had meant to replace it but not got around to it. Then I went around making sure all the doors were closed. I set fire to the living room curtains first. Then the Sunday paper, with all the different sections. I arranged most of them on the floor around the legs of the chair he was sitting in. I lit a cigarette from the packet on the coffee table and laid it carefully on the newspaper directly underneath his hand, which was hanging down over the arm of the chair.

Then, I crept back through the kitchen. The blaze was crackling around me and the smoke was already making it hard to see two feet in front of me. I took the key from the inside of the back door and stepped out into the garden. I didn't know air could taste so good. I closed the door behind me and locked it with the key before pushing the key back under the door.

The back door was the most obvious escape route from the living room, and I was sure he would try to get out that way. He wouldn't see the key because of the smoke. And with any luck, the police would think he had knocked the key to the floor in his panic to get away.

After I ran off, I stood at the corner of the road and watched as the first licks of black smoke came snaking out of the building. My heart was still pounding, my thoughts racing. Only when the front door opened and a woman came out with her hand to her mouth, did I stop to think about the people in the other flats.

I didn't want anything bad to happen to them.

I'm not a monster.

As luck would have it, the only person who got hurt was *him*. Really, things couldn't have worked out any better.

I spent the night pacing the streets, my nerves jangling. Every time I heard a car behind me, I thought it was the police coming to arrest me.

It was six o'clock in the morning before I snuck back home while you were all asleep. It is the first day of the Easter holidays. I knew no one would be up early. No one heard me hook the ladder down and climb back up to the loft.

Through the kitchen camera, I watch you talking to the kids. You are telling them that you can't set off to Cornwall until later, as there is a problem with the electrical wiring in the house. You say you don't want to leave it as it is while you are away, in case of fire. Something flickers in your pale face when you say the word *fire*. Then it is gone.

You have called Mel's brother, Gaz, in to do the wiring, and that makes me grit my teeth until they hurt. Gaz calls himself a handyman, but he is useless. Why didn't you ask me to do it? I always did everything around the house.

I have calmed down a little by the time Gaz arrives. Now Croissant Man is out of the way, it is only a matter of time before you come running back to me. And once I am back home, there will be no more calls to Gaz.

Also, I am looking forward to having the house to myself while you are all in Cornwall. Sleeping in my own bed. Taking a bath.

When Gaz switches off the electrics, the cameras stop working, so I put down my phone and think about us. We have been through the worst. From now on, everything will be better.

This has been a test of our marriage, a test of me. And I have proved myself. There is nothing I will not do for you. For us.

Till death do us part.

Chapter Nineteen

KATE: Monday afternoon,
twenty-two days after the split

Gaz is starting to pack up his tools when Kate says, 'Oh, there is one more thing, Gaz.'

She leads him up to the landing, where they look up at the hatch to the loft.

'Are you sure?' he says, when she explains what she wants. He looks doubtful. 'All that useful space?'

'I don't use it,' says Kate. 'And there's always a draught coming from there. And now the squirrels with their endless scratching. It gives me the creeps.'

So Gaz gets started. And when he finishes, the ceiling is plastered over so smoothly you can't see there was ever a hatch there.

An hour later, Kate packs up the car with her still arguing children and their bags and the cat box containing a furious Sid. She double-locks the door behind her.

After the pure grief of yesterday and last night, she feels strangely calm. Numb. As if she has felt so much, so strongly, she has now run out of feelings.

As she watches the house grow smaller in the rear-view mirror, she wonders vaguely how long it will take Jack to realize the plastic water bottles in the corner of the loft are all empty. And the boxes of crisps and biscuits, too. And that the hatch opening has been sealed shut.

She thinks of the smooth white walls that slope right down to the floor. The ceiling that is too low to stand up straight.

It is a bit like a tomb, up there in the loft.

By the time she turns the corner, the kids have stopped arguing and the house is no longer in view.

Kate wipes her mind clear, as if she is cleaning a whiteboard.

Then she turns the radio on and settles back into her seat.

She has a long trip ahead.

If you've enjoyed this Quick Read title,
why not try another Tammy Cohen book?

Keep reading for an extract from

They All Fall Down

1

Hannah

Charlie cut her wrists last week with a shard of caramelized sugar.

We'd made the sugar sheets together in the clinic's kitchen earlier in the day, under Joni's beady-eyed supervision.

'Yours are thick enough to do yourself an injury,' I'd said to Charlie, as a joke.

'I wonder if that's what gave her the idea,' Odelle commented afterwards, pointedly.

After Charlie died, *Bake Off* went on the banned-programmes list.

I don't feel guilty, though, because I don't think Charlie killed herself. Just as I don't think poor Sofia killed herself. In a high-suicide-risk psych clinic like this, people die all the time. It's one of the clinic's USPs. That's what makes it so easy for a killer to hide here, in plain sight. That and the fact that the only witnesses are us, and no one believes a word we say.

You don't have to be mad to live here but . . . oh, hang on, yes, you do.

I'm frightened. I'm frightened that I'm right and I'll be next. I'm even more frightened that I'm wrong, in which case I'm as crazy as they all think I am. Shut away in here, the only escape is in my own head. But what if my own head's the most dangerous place to be?

Stella comes into my room and lies across the end of my bed without speaking. Her skin is stretched tight over the sharp points of her cheeks and I can't look at it for fear it might tear.

'It's not true,' I tell her.

My room is at the side of the building. I am sitting by the window in the beige armchair, looking out across the rose garden to where a half-hearted rain is drip, drip, dripping from the flat roof of the dance studio and running down the wall of folding glass doors. All the furniture in my room is a variation on beige. Ecru. Biscuit. Stone. The whole of the upstairs is the colour of a surgical bandage. To avoid us getting over-stimulated, I imagine. Not much chance of that in here.

Stella turns her head so her wide blue eyes are fixed on mine. The necklace she always wears has fallen to the side so that the tiny silver cat seems to be nestling into the duvet.

'How do you know?' she says at last, in her soft, smoker's voice.

I frown at her.

'Come on,' I say. 'It's Charlie.'

'Was,' she says. And starts to cry.

The Meadows is an old Georgian-style country house, complete with ivy growing across the front and elegant floor-to-ceiling sash windows. From the semicircular gravel drive at the front you might imagine yourself on the set of a Jane Austen adaptation where at any moment the grand front door will burst open to disgorge a gaggle of giggling young women in bonnets. But drive around to the car park behind the house and the impression is ruined by a large modern extension stuck on to the back, giving the overall effect of a stylish man with a bad toupee.

All the consulting rooms and the day room and admin and therapy rooms are in the old part, while the cafeteria and the bedrooms are in the new bit. Sofia told me once the old part was haunted, but I've never sensed anything weird. Mind you, I was so numb when I first arrived a ghost could have climbed right on to my lap and I wouldn't have registered it. The thing about staying in a place like this, where we have group therapy twice a day and keep journals detailing our every thought, is that we're so busy gazing inwards we're blind to what's going on all around us.

Which might explain how two women have been killed and nobody seems to have noticed but me.

The art therapy room is at the back of the old

house with two huge windows giving out on to the car park and beyond to the flower garden and then the vegetable plot. The jewel in The Meadows' crown – the manicured lawn leading down to a lake that is disproportionately large and deep, a legacy of an earlier, grander incarnation of the house – is hidden from view by the ugly jut of the new extension on the left.

It is ten o'clock on Wednesday morning and we are at art therapy. Laura gets out the poster paints and asks us to do a self-portrait. The last time we did this exercise she gave us mirrors made of plastic instead of glass, so our reflections were smudgy, like we were looking at ourselves through smoke. 'Sorry,' she said when we complained. 'Regulations. You know how it is.' But today is different.

'I want you to paint yourselves the way you see yourselves when you close your eyes,' she says. 'Where are you? What are you doing? What are you wearing? Don't overthink it. And don't pay any heed to the camera. Just forget it's there.'

The film crew – which most of the time consists only of director/presenter Justin Carter and his cameraman Drew Abbott – have been installed at the clinic for the last seven weeks, just one week less than me. I arrived on the third Monday in January, auspiciously known as Blue Monday, which is officially the most depressing day of the year, although, as you can imagine, competition for that title is fierce in here. Justin and Drew turned up the following week in an SUV loaded with equipment which they carted through from the rain-soaked car park, propping the door to reception open so an icy draught swept through the building and Bridget Ashworth, the clinic's frowning admin manager, bustled about adjusting thermostats and ordering cleaning staff to mop up muddy footprints.

They're calling it a fly-on-the-wall documentary. But Dr Roberts spun it differently: 'An important film in breaking down the taboos surrounding mental illness,' he said. 'Of course, you are all perfectly entitled to opt out of the filming and at any stage you can be retrospectively edited out. But just think what your example could mean to a young woman going through what you've been through, feeling there's nobody out there who could possibly understand.'

On the first day, Justin said, 'Just imagine we're not really here.'

'That's how most of us ended up in this place,' Charlie told him. 'For seeing things that aren't there, or not seeing things that are there. You could seriously set back our recovery.'

Justin had smiled without committing himself to laughing, just in case it wasn't appropriate, not understanding that appropriateness is something you leave at the door in here.

Today, in my painting, I am sitting in the low blue velvet chair in Emily's room. Through the sash window behind me the sky is navy and I put in a perfectly round yellowy-white moon so it's obvious it's night-time. I am looking at something over to the right, out of sight. I'm wearing my pale blue dressing gown. My face is a pink blur, streaked with black because I didn't wait long enough for the paint to dry before trying to do the eyes.

'Nice dress,' Laura says when she comes round to look. 'Is that in your house? Your bedroom, maybe?'

I nod. I don't want to tell her the truth because when I talk about Emily it gets noted down in a book and then I have to talk about it at Group. And then Dr Roberts will cock his head to one side and write something in his notebook and I might have to stay here longer. So I don't tell her that the me in the picture is looking at the right-hand corner of Emily's room, where her cot used to be.

Stella's painting is all black, except for a tiny figure at the bottom, naked apart from her long, yellow hair, which reaches almost to the floor. Laura looks at it for a long time and then puts her hand on Stella's narrow shoulder and squeezes before moving on to someone else.

Since Charlie died, all Stella's paintings have been black.

As usual, Odelle has painted herself hugely fat. She's wearing the same black top and skinny jeans the real Odelle has on today and is looking into a mirror in which a slimline version of herself is

102

reflected back. Or maybe it's the other way around and the slim Odelle is the real one and the fat one the reflection. Either way, it's just another variation of Odelle's sole enduring theme. Herself and her body.

'It's very . . . narrative, Odelle,' says Laura. Odelle glances towards the camera at the back of the room, wanting to be sure they are capturing this. 'But just once, I'd love to see you really let rip. This exercise is about here' – Laura taps her chest lightly – 'not about here,' tapping her head.

The mild rebuke sets Odelle's bottom lip trembling. Odelle tends to fixate on people. That's one of the reasons she's in here. That and the fact she weighs around eighty-five pounds. When Charlie first arrived, Odelle apparently fixated on her too for a short while, following her around, sitting too close to her at dinner and on the sofa in the lounge. But mostly it's authority figures she goes for. Roberts is basically God as far as Odelle is concerned, and Laura comes a close second. Odelle's always loitering in the art room after class, offering to help clear away or asking for extra, one-to-one help.

The Meadows believes in niche therapy. We have people who come in to cure us through horticulture, music, baking and movement. Last week, Grace, the aptly named movement therapist, had us fling ourselves around the dance studio pretending to be leaves blown about by the wind and

Odelle actually cried. 'I feel so insignificant,' she said. Judith said the reason Odelle got upset was probably because she really did get blown about by the wind, on account of weighing so little.

Basically, nothing happens in here that can't be turned into some kind of therapy. There's even recreational therapy, which really means watching TV. Charlie and I had a running joke about that. Instead of asking if I was going to dinner, she'd say, 'Are you coming to eating therapy?' One time, when I was late down to breakfast, I said I'd been doing some 'pooing therapy' and we laughed for about ten minutes, until Odelle told us we were being childish and also 'insensitive' to all the people in here who 'can't find much to laugh about'.

But Laura is the therapist people get closest to. She used to be a nurse in her younger days, and she still emits that I-can-make-you-better aura. She has her own little office at the back of the art room, with a fan heater and a kettle and several different types of tea, and you can pop in there and curl up on the armchair and wrap yourself up in the soft woollen tartan throw for a chat without feeling like what you say will be noted down in your file somewhere. Laura can be a little bit new-agey. For those who are into that sort of thing, she offers informal meditation or relaxation therapy, which is basically hypnosis. Charlie used to love it in there. 'It's the only part of the clinic where I can be myself,' she told me once. Odelle nips in there at any opportunity. She installs herself in the armchair, with the tartan blanket wrapped around all those other layers she habitually wears, and discusses her favourite subject. Namely, herself.

Laura spends a few moments murmuring something to Nina, who is slumped in front of a piece of paper which is blank apart from a faintly drawn oval. Last week in art she produced seven paintings in one class, her brush flying over the paper, colours bleeding into one another, but today she can hardly summon the energy to lift her stick of charcoal.

Frannie is crying again, tears tracking slowly down her cheeks, and she brushes them away as if she hardly notices them. Her painting has two figures in it, which, strictly speaking, is cheating, but no one is judging. Firstly, there's a huge face with a long, fine nose and a small, full mouth and massive green eyes. The face is Frannie's, and in one of the eyes is another face. It's too small for the features to be identifiable but the black curls mark it out as Charlie.

'Because she's in your thoughts?' asks Laura.

My chest feels tight when I look at the straight brown bob Frannie has given herself in her portrait, hanging just below her chin. The real Frannie is wearing a blue-and-white striped beanie hat, but underneath it her hair is sparse and thin with bald patches that break your heart, vulnerable as the soft part on a newborn baby's head.

My baby was called Emily.

And now I don't want to paint any more.

Later on, in Evening Group, we start, as always, by going round each one of us in the circle, reporting back on whether we've achieved the two goals we each set ourselves this morning. Mine were to start reading a proper book, as opposed to the celebrity magazines which are all I've read for the last two months, and to wash my hair. I failed at the first, the letters moving across the page like lines of tiny ants. But in the second goal I can claim some success, having dragged myself, finally, into the shower, so that my hair, while still a tangled mess, is at least clean for the first time in days. I hate myself for the glow of pleasure I feel when Dr Roberts says, 'Well *done*, Hannah,' and everyone gives me a round of applause, as if I've climbed Mount Kilimanjaro or something.

After about half an hour we go back to talking about Charlie. Odelle shares a story about when she first arrived here and was missing her family and had just gone through her first meal with someone sitting next to her monitoring everything that went into her mouth and was curled up on her bed, crying into her pillow – Odelle holds a hand to her face to demonstrate, visibly moved by her own story – and Charlie knocked on her door and sat on the end of the bed and chatted to her, and even made her laugh. That was the thing about Charlie. She could say things to make you laugh so hard your tea came out of your nose. Then she'd go back to her room and make bite marks on her own arm. Of all the people I've met in my life, she was the one who was most forgiving of others – and the least forgiving of herself.

'But she didn't kill herself,' I say, when it's my turn to speak.

Dr Roberts sits back in his seat with one leg crossed over the other at the knee and one elbow hooked over the back of the chair. He has a pen in his hand and he clicks the end in and out as he listens, and nods. His eyes are narrowed so I can't see them, but I know they are blue in some lights and green in others. His hair, brown but liberally threaded with silver, is swept back from his face, although a lock often falls over his left eye when he gets animated. His close-cropped beard is equal measures of silver and brown, and when he smiles, two dimples appear in his cheeks and the lines around his eyes concertina into folds a person could get lost in.

The transference rate – that thing where patients end up in love with their shrinks – is pretty high in our clinic.

'It's a very interesting theory, Hannah.' His voice is warm and honey-coated. 'But you know – we all knew – that Charlie was deeply, chronically depressed. Just because we loved her doesn't mean we could help her. It's inevitable that we all feel some sense of failure that we couldn't do more, and failure is a damned uncomfortable feeling. It's far preferable to imagine she was done away with against her will, because that's not anything we could have prevented or seen coming. But the fact is, we weren't responsible. There's nothing anyone could have done.'

'Yes, we have to forgive ourselves,' adds Odelle.

I look around the circle, where twelve women sit on chairs, one leg twisted around the other, heads bowed, hands fidgeting. I see Frannie plucking at her almost non-existent eyelashes. She studies a hair and then pops it into her mouth. I see Stella staring impassively ahead through her widely stretched eyes. She's wearing a powder-blue dress today that has a tight bodice and a flared skirt. I try not to look at the waist, made artificially tiny by the removal of a rib, nor at the painful swell of her surgically enhanced breasts. I see Odelle, who layers clothes on to her body like she is making papier mâché, leaning forward earnestly, sniffing for approval like a blind laboratory rat. I see Judith and Nina and the eight other inmates – service users, as we're officially known – and Justin and Drew, shadowing our every move with the camera. And though my back is towards the door, in my head I see, through the safety-glass panel behind me, across the hallway and up the sweeping wooden staircase that leads to the plush consulting rooms, to where Dr Chakraborty, the clinic's deputy director, sits in his office, reading through notes with his sad, brown eyes, while downstairs in the therapy rooms I see Laura and Grace and the other part-time therapists. At the back of the staircase, through the door that leads to the new building, and the cafeteria and kitchen and the Mindfulness Area and the tiny staffroom where the medicines are kept, I see Joni and Darren, the psychiatric nurses, clutching their notebooks, and Bridget Ashworth, the clinic's brisk admin manager, and the well-meaning volunteers and the kitchen staff and the orderlies. All the people charged with keeping us safe. And then my gaze is pulled back here again and I see Dr Oliver Roberts, guru, Svengali, saint, sage, saviour.

Murderer?

It could be him. It could be any of them.

But it definitely happened.

I'd have to be crazy to make a thing like that up.

Towards the end of our session, at about seven thirty, I slip away while the others are still stacking up the chairs. After eight weeks here, the grandeur of the hallway, with its glass chandelier and vast oil painting of the earl whose home this once was, no longer comes as a surprise. No one uses the front entrance anyway, unless they're an important dignitary or there's a fundraising event going on. The main entrance is round the back in the new wing, where a receptionist checks in visitors and politely searches their bags under the gaze of a smiling Oliver Roberts clad in a formal academic gown in the act of being awarded some honour or other.

But when I go through the door that divides the old building from the new, I don't go straight ahead, past the Mindfulness Area and the blond wood of the cafeteria, to where the vibrant orange reception sofa calls a cheerful greeting, as if to reassure visitors this is not a place conducive to dark thoughts. Instead, I take the first door on the left, which leads to the stairwell, with its muted oatmeal walls, and hurry on up to the bedrooms.

My room is the first on the left, but I walk straight past it and continue down the corridor, with its framed photographs of nature – a close-up of dew on a blade of grass, a feather floating in a muddy puddle, sunlight glittering through a canopy of green leaves. The photographs are caulked to the walls so that we can't take them off and use them against ourselves, or each other. The very last room is Charlie's room.

How many times have I made this journey between my room and hers over the last eight weeks? I'm surprised my feet haven't made indentations in the strip wood flooring. Yet now I feel strange and unease prickles at the back of my neck. I glance up into the eye of a CCTV camera.

The camera has always been there, but it is the first time I've really noticed it. Its unblinking stare makes me anxious.

Our doors don't have locks. For obvious reasons. Even so, I'm surprised when Charlie's handle turns. I hesitate before stepping inside.

I've been steeling myself to find her room cleared and emptied of all the things that made it Charlie's. But it's all still there – the blown-up photograph of her and her little nieces in her parents' garden, their three heads dark against an explosion of yellow hibiscus, the lifesize cardboard cutout of Ryan Gosling given to her by an ex-workmate, the old-fashioned patchwork quilt on the bed, a riot of colour amidst the oppressive beigeness.

Yet whereas Charlie was notoriously untidy, with paperbacks piled precariously on the floor next to her bed, and jeans and sweaters strewn over the chair or heaped on the floor, the room has been meticulously tidied. The desk has been cleared of old newspapers and magazines and empty crisp packets, its white surface bland and clean. The bed, which was always messy, as if someone had just that minute got out of it, is now perfectly made, the quilt pulled taut.

I put a hand on the pillow and it feels smooth and unnaturally cold to the touch, like a bar of soap, and I snatch it back. I slide open a desk drawer. Empty, apart from a few pens and a pad of paper. The wardrobe has no door, its edges rounded in case anyone should decide to string themselves up from a sharp corner. I almost cry out when I see her fuchsia cashmere cardigan hanging on one of the weirdly shaped cardboard hangers, suspended from a rail designed to break under 'undue weight'. How she loved that cardigan. She'd told me about a decluttering handbook her mother had given her in a not-so-subtle hint. Charlie had refused to read it on principle but had grudgingly flicked through, taking away from it just one thing – that you should only hang on to things that spark joy. 'This here is my joy-sparking cardigan,' she said to me.

Now it hangs on the clothes hanger, its empty arms drooping.

The absence of joy is palpable. Rather, again, I have that sense of unease, of being watched.

Charlie has a corner room, and I cross to the window on the back wall that looks out over the sloping lawn and, at the very bottom, the dark smudge of the lake. There are days when the sun is reflected on the surface of the water, making the lake appear to be lit up from within. But not today.

A radiator runs underneath the window. On especially cold days Charlie would throw a cushion down on the floor and sit cross-legged on the carpet with her back to the radiator. 'I can never get warm enough,' she once told me. 'I'm like a chicken breast that hasn't quite thawed out, with a hard, frozen bit in the middle that refuses to defrost.'

I drop to the floor and assume her position, trying to inhabit her skin, to feel what she felt. Did she really sit here that last day with the heat against her back and think about how best to slice into her wrist, the right angle, the right point? Is it possible I could have got it – got her – so wrong?

There was a time I was sure of my own judgement, trusted in myself. But that was before.

I hug my knees into my chest and rock gently for a while. Sometimes this soothes me, but there is something about this room without Charlie in it that makes me anxious.

I hear the soft thud of footsteps outside, and voices drawing closer.

'We've cleared as much as we could, and I don't mind telling you the place was a pigsty. But there's a limit to how much we can do before the relatives turn up.'

The woman says 'relatives' as though it's something not quite nice. I stop rocking abruptly, putting my hand down to steady me. My fingers brush against a piece of paper tucked away behind the pipe of the radiator which the cleaners must have missed. The footsteps stop outside the door and my mouth goes dry as I recognize Dr Roberts' familiar baritone, sounding unusually clipped and impatient.

'With any luck, they won't stay long. Quick in–out, then we can get all her stuff bagged up. We've a new one arriving a week on Monday.'

113

The door handle turns and I've just time to snatch up the scrap of paper and stuff it up the sleeve of my sweatshirt before the door bursts open.

I scramble to my feet, my heart hammering.

'Right. Let's have a quick check over . . . Hannah! What are you doing in here?'

Instantly, Dr Roberts reverts to his usual slow drawl and I wonder if the woman with him, who I now recognize as Bridget Ashworth, has also clocked the change in his voice.

Bridget Ashworth has a severe brown bob with a grey re-growth line along the parting and glasses with purple frames and a dark wool jacket with what appears to be a single thick white cat hair on the shoulder. She clutches her lanyard and blinks behind her lenses as if she has surprised a wild fox rifling through her kitchen bin, while I shift from foot to foot.

Who would believe I used to give presentations to roomfuls of people, scanning the crowd and making deliberate eye contact with random strangers?

Now I keep my eyes on the carpet, but still, as I mumble some story about needing to feel close to Charlie, I sense Bridget Ashworth's disapproving gaze crawl over me.

Even when I get back to the safety of my own room, I'm still scratching, trying to get it off.

**READ THE COMPLETE BOOK
– AVAILABLE NOW**

About Quick Reads

Quick Reads are brilliant short new books written by bestselling writers. They are perfect for regular readers wanting a fast and satisfying read, but they are also ideal for adults who are discovering reading for pleasure for the first time.

Since Quick Reads was founded in 2006, over 4.5 million copies of more than a hundred titles have been sold or distributed. Quick Reads are available in paperback, in ebook and from your local library.

To find out more about Quick Reads titles, visit
www.readingagency.org.uk/quickreads

Quick Reads is part of The Reading Agency, the leading charity inspiring people of all ages and all backgrounds to read for pleasure and empowerment. Working with our partners, our aim is to make reading accessible to everyone. The Reading Agency is funded by the Arts Council.

www.readingagency.org.uk Tweet us @readingagency

The Reading Agency Ltd • Registered number: 3904882 (England & Wales) Registered charity number: 1085443 (England & Wales) Registered Office: Free Word Centre, 60 Farringdon Road, London, EC1R 3GA The Reading Agency is supported using public funding by Arts Council England.

We would like to thank all our funders and a range of private donors who believe in the value of our work.

LOTTERY FUNDED

THE
READING
AGENCY

has something for everyone

Stories to make you laugh

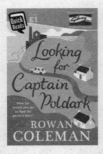

Stories to make you feel good

Stories to take you to another place

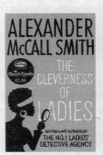

Stories about real life

ANDY McNAB
AUTHOR OF *BRAVO TWO ZERO*
TODAY
everything
changes

Only £1
Street Cat
Bob
HOW ONE MAN AND A CAT SAVED
EACH OTHER'S LIVES. A TRUE STORY
A SPECIAL QUICK READS EDITION
JAMES BOWEN

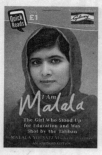

I Am Malala
The Girl Who Stood Up
for Education and Was
Shot by the Taliban
MALALA YOUSAFZAI
AN ABRIDGED EDITION

Stories to take you to another time

£1
OUT OF
THE DARK
ADÈLE GERAS

Only £1
A CRUEL
FATE
LINDSEY
DAVIS

Only £1
A
DREADFUL
MURDER
THE MYSTERIOUS DEATH
OF CAROLINE LUARD
MINETTE WALTERS
THE NUMBER ONE BESTSELLING AUTHOR

Stories to make you turn the pages

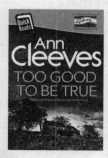

Ann
Cleeves
TOO GOOD
TO BE TRUE

£1
DEAD
SIMPLE
EIGHT KILLER READS
FROM EIGHT
BESTSELLING AUTHORS
EDITED BY HARRY BINGHAM

£1
Amanda Craig
THE
OTHER
SIDE OF
YOU

£1
ONE FALSE
MOVE
DREDA SAY MITCHELL

For a complete list of titles visit
www.readingagency.org.uk/quickreads

Available in paperback, ebook
and from your local library

Why not start a reading group?

If you have enjoyed this book, why not share your next Quick Read with friends, colleagues, or neighbours?

The Reading Agency also runs **Reading Groups for Everyone** which helps you discover and share new books. Find a reading group near you, or register a group you already belong to and get free books and offers from publishers at **readinggroups.org**

There is a free toolkit with lots of ideas to help you run a Quick Reads reading group at **www.readingagency.org.uk/quickreads**

Share your experiences of your group on Twitter

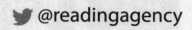 @readingagency

Continuing your reading journey

As well as Quick Reads, The Reading Agency runs lots of programmes to help keep you and your family reading.

Reading Ahead invites you to pick six reads and record your reading in a diary to get a certificate **readingahead.org.uk**

World Book Night is an annual celebration of reading and books on 23 April **worldbooknight.org**

Chatterbooks children's reading groups and the **Summer Reading Challenge** inspire children to read more and share the books they love **readingagency.org.uk/children**